Scary Night Visitors

A Story for Children with Bedtime Fears

by Irene Wineman Marcus
& Paul Marcus, Ph.D.

illustrated by Susan Jeschke

MAGINATION PRESS • WASHINGTON, DC

to Raphael and Gabriela

Library of Congress Cataloging-in-Publication Data
Marcus, Irene Wineman.
     Scary night visitors : a story for children with bedtime fears /
by Irene Wineman Marcus and Paul Marcus ; illustrated by Susan
Jeschke.
          p.   cm.
     Summary: When Davey realizes that his scary nighttime visitors
are really his unacceptable angry feelings about his little sister,
projected into the outside world, he feels free to express his anger
in a healthy way.
     ISBN 0-945354-26-6.—ISBN 0-945354-25-8 (pbk.)
     [1. Fear—Fiction.   2. Anger—Fiction.   3. Bedtime—Fiction.
4. Brothers and sisters—Fiction.]   I. Marcus, Paul.   II. Jeschke,
Susan, ill.   III. Title.
PZ7.M329Sc   1990
[E]—dc20   90-41919
                                                                CIP
                                                                 AC

Manufactured in the United States of America

10 9 8 7 6 5 4 3

Introduction for Parents

Many children have bedtime fears, starting as young as two years old and continuing for several years. Using a lively storyline children will identify with, *Scary Night Visitors* shows why they have these fears. Helping children understand the origin of the fear, rather than just explaining, for example, the ghost as wind howling through the trees or the monster as clothes draped on the chair, makes it less likely that one fear will be replaced by another.

This story shows the scary visitors to be the child's own unacceptable angry feelings, disowned and projected onto the outside world. The anger, which in this story is directed toward the younger sister (although it could be the mother, father, or anyone the child loves), is unacceptable because of the child's worry and fear that the bad wishes could come true. The feeling that wishes and thoughts will actually happen is common to us all at some time. Children, particularly, feel that they are powerful and magic enough to make things come true. By realizing that the wishes are not all powerful, children can feel safe enough to be angry. By experiencing their own anger safely, they will feel less need to disown and project it, and can thus gain control over their scary visitors.

Hearing this story repeatedly, and exploring with parents (or therapists or counselors) the kinds of things that make them angry, children will gradually learn that they can think, wish, and feel freely. They will then do so without worrying about bad consequences.

"Good night, sleep tight," said Mommy as she turned off the light and closed the door.

Before Davey could get his head under the covers, his scary visitors arrived.

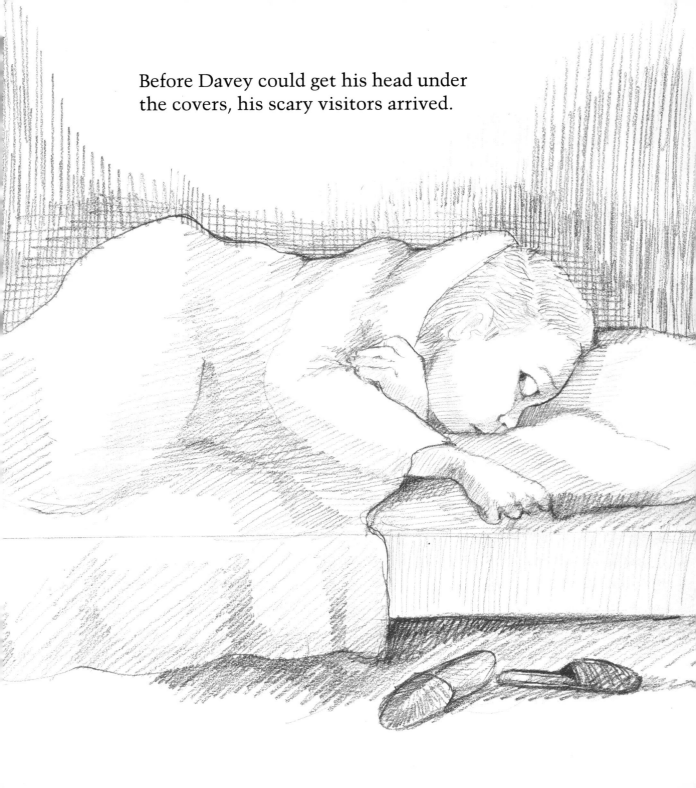

There was the big fierce lion he called Leethul, the big fierce tiger he called Tera, and the "Something"—who didn't have a name—but was the biggest and fiercest of them all.

Davey screamed for his Mommy.

As soon as she came back, Leethul, Tera and the Something got smaller. The bigger the hug and the bigger the kiss from Mommy, the smaller Leethul, Tera and the Something became.

Then Mommy left again.

The dark again got darker, and the visitors again got bigger and fiercer.

Davey shivered and shook. He tried to remember the ways to get rid of his visitors.

"Be a lion tamer," Daddy had said.

"Imagine Tera is just a cuddly pussy cat," said Mommy,

"and the Something just the shadow of the clothes on
your chair." Davey tried, but none of it worked.

The next morning Davey had forgotten all about his visitors. He hurried outside to play. He threw his ball as high as he could. Maybe it would hit the branches of the chestnut tree.

"Nope, not high enough." Down came the ball, and
along came his sister, Patti. She picked up the ball and
ran off with it. "That's mine! Give it to me!" Davey yelled.

Mommy called from the doorway,
"Share with your sister. Why don't
you play catch together?"

"I don't want to share and I don't want to play catch,"
Davey answered. He ran over, pushed Patti, and
grabbed the ball. "Grr . . . It's mine," he said.

Mommy ran out. "You can be angry with your sister, but you cannot push her. Go to your room." Davey scowled. "You can scowl and growl in your room," said Mommy.

As soon as he opened the door, Davey saw he had
visitors. Leethul, Tera and the Something all let out
a terrible roar.

Davey remembered that Mommy had
said he could scowl and growl in his
room. So Davey tried a long low growl.
The visitors looked at him and he
looked at them.

Then they all roared together!

Davey smiled. "Now I'm an angry lion. I can scare Mommy so she won't ever make me share."

Davey growled again.
"I'm an angry tiger.
I can chase Patti away."

Davey looked around and saw the Something. He pushed out his chest and stood as tall as he could. He shouted, "I'm an angry Something!"

Suddenly Davey wondered if he could *really* make
something happen just by wishing it. He decided to try.
"Move!" he commanded. But his fire engine stood still.
He decided to try another wish.

He looked out his window and saw Patti.
He stretched out his arm and said, "Go away!"
Patti ran out of the yard.

Before Davey could begin worrying if she would ever come back, she returned with her favorite teddy bear. "One more try," Davey thought. He stretched out his arm again and said, "Disappear!"

But Patti just kept playing.

Davey felt disappointed. It would be great to have thoughts and wishes that always came true.

But sometimes he changed
his mind and liked to play
with Patti. Davey smiled
with relief.

Davey thought, "Even if my angry wishes don't come true, I can still think them, because that can't hurt anyone. I'll still get into trouble if I do mean things." "But I can feel just as big, mean and angry as I want!"

That night Davey didn't hide under his covers. He sat up in bed, looked around the room, and whispered into the darkness, "Good-bye, Tera. Good-bye, Leethul. Good-bye Something." No one answered.

And no one visited, except Mommy and Daddy with
a good night kiss.